For Helen
S.P.

For Freya and Tom
A.P.

First published 2017 by Nosy Crow Ltd
The Crow's Nest, Baden Place, Crosby Row, London, SE1 1YW
www.nosycrow.com

ISBN 978 1 78800 011 6 (HB)
ISBN 978 1 78800 012 3 (PB)

Nosy Crow and associated logos are trademarks and/or registered trademarks of Nosy Crow Ltd

Text © Simon Puttock 2017
Illustrations © Ali Pye 2017

The right of Simon Puttock to be identified as the author and Ali Pye to be identified
as the illustrator of this work has been asserted.

A CIP catalogue record for this book is available from the British Library.

Printed in China

Papers used by Nosy Crow are made from wood grown in sustainable forests.

1 3 5 7 9 8 6 4 2 (HB)
1 3 5 7 9 8 6 4 2 (PB)

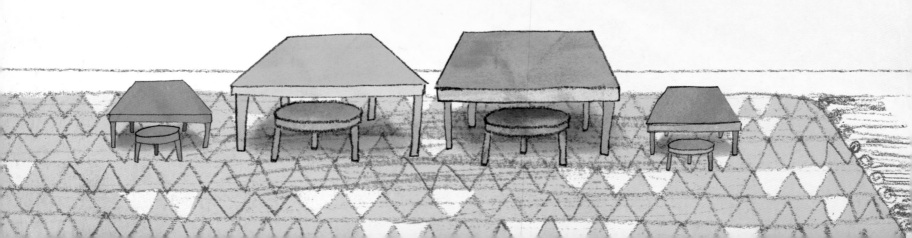

CAT LEARNS TO LISTEN AT
MOONLIGHT SCHOOL

SIMON PUTTOCK

Illustrated by ALI PYE

nosy
crow

This is Miss Moon's Moonlight School
for all the wee small creatures of the night.

The night bell had rung,
    but Bat
        and Cat
            and Owl
                and Mouse were not there,
                    because . . .

. . . they were all OUTSIDE!

"Tonight," said Miss Moon, "we are going on a nature walk to see what interesting things we can find.

Now, listen carefully, everyone – please
stay in pairs and, most importantly of all,
NOBODY must wander off!"

Owl and Bat lined up ready to go.

"Cat!" whispered Mouse.
"You have to hold my paw!"

But Cat had NOT been listening –
she was busy fiddling
with her clipboard.

"Now," said Miss Moon,
"has anyone found anything yet?"

"I have found the moon!" said Mouse.

"And I have found MISS Moon," said Owl,
feeling rather clever.

"I can see a cloud that looks like a cake," said Bat.

But Cat did not say anything. She was still not listening – she was busy doodling a flower.

Then Mouse found a special starry leaf.

And Bat found a swirly snail.

Owl THOUGHT he found
a swirly snail too, but it
was only a stone, after all.

"A stone still counts,"
said Miss Moon. "ESPECIALLY
one that looks like a snail.
Now, Cat, dear, what can you find?"

But Cat was STILL not listening.
She was slipping through the shadows.
She had found a flittery thing and
she was following it!

"Cat, dear?" said Miss Moon loudly.

"Miss Moon," said Mouse, "I think
Cat has WANDERED OFF!"

"Then we must find her
AT ONCE," said Miss Moon.
"Let's all shout for Cat!"

Everyone shouted for Cat
as loudly as they could.

But . . .

. . . Cat did not hear.
She had wandered too far away!

The flittery thing settled on a flower.

"Oh!" said Cat. "You're a FIREFLY!
Miss Moon will be ever so pleased.
Look, Miss Moon, I've found a firefly!"

But Miss Moon was not THERE!
And nor were Bat or Owl or Mouse.
And THEN the firefly flittered off
and Cat was all alone!

"Oh no!" said Cat. "Where can everyone be?

Miss Moon?

MISS MOOOOOOOOON?"

"Listen!" said Owl.
"What's that?"

"A noise," said Mouse.

"A noise that sounds
like Cat," said Bat.

"Everyone follow me!"
said Miss Moon.

First, Owl found Cat's clipboard.
"It's a CLUE!" said Miss Moon.

And THEN Bat found
Cat's pencil. "ANOTHER clue!"
he shouted excitedly.

And then Mouse found a third clue –
a trail of paw prints leading off into
the bushes – and THEN . . .

"THERE you are, Cat," said Miss Moon.
"Weren't you listening before?
Don't you know you must NEVER
run off like that?"

"But I saw a flittery THING," said Cat,
"and then it was a firefly, but nobody
was there and I was LOST and,
oh, poor, poor MEEEE!"

"You must promise," said Miss Moon,
"that you will never wander off like that again.
Do you promise, Cat, dear?"

"Oh yes," said Cat.
"I do promise. I truly do!"

When everyone was safely back at Moonlight School, Miss Moon said, "Now, can anyone remember some of the interesting things we found?"

"We found the moon," said Mouse, "and a special starry leaf."

"And a cloud that looked like a cake," said Bat, "and a swirly snail."

"I NEARLY found a snail too," said Owl, "but it was a stone. And, oh, oh, oh! We found THREE CLUES!"

"Is that EVERYTHING we found?"
asked Miss Moon.

"No!" shouted Mouse and Owl
and Bat. "After THAT we found
the Most Important Thing . . .

. . . we found Cat!"